Surprise, Stegosaurus!

Based on text by Dawn Bentley
Illustrated by Karen Carr

SMITHSONIAN INSTITUTION

Published by Soundprints™, an imprint of Palm Publishing,
Norwalk, Connecticut USA
www.palmkids.com

Editors: Barbie Heit & Samantha Schlemm
Book design: Katie Sears & Scott Variano

First Edition 2012
10 9 8 7 6 5 4 3 2 1

Acknowledgements:

Carol LeBlanc, *Vice President*, Smithsonian Enterprises
Brigid Ferraro, *Director of Licensing*, Smithsonian Enterprises

Our special thanks to Ellen Nanney and Kealy Wilson at the Smithsonian
Institution's Licensing Division for their help in the creation of this book.
Our very special thanks to Dr. Mike Brett-Surman of the Smithsonian
Institution's National Museum of Natural History for his curatorial review
of this title.

Library of Congress Control Number: 2012940524

Table of Contents

Good Morning 5

Being Careful 10

Danger! 14

The Search Continues 20

New Babies 25

Glossary 28

About the Stegosaurus 29

Good Morning

One morning, Stegosaurus wakes up near her nest of eggs. She looks around for danger and gets ready to start her day.

Stegosaurus cannot stay by
her nest all day. She is hungry
and must leave to find food.

With luck, her eggs will be safe until she returns.

She looks for something to
eat and snips off a piece of **fern**
growing nearby.

Stegosaurus has a toothless **beak**, which means she doesn't chew. She swallows the fern whole.

Being Careful

Stegosaurus continues her search for more food. Small animals jump out of her way.

She must be careful, too. There
may be **predators** nearby.

Stegosaurus stays alert as she drinks from a stream. She knows sometimes an **Allosaurus** hides near the stream. Stegosaurus is strong, but not very fast. Allosaurus is not an easy predator to defeat.

Danger!

Other dinosaurs splash in the water. A **Brachiosaurus** eats leaves from a tall tree.

Everything is calm, until
another dinosaur cries out in fear.
Stegosaurus knows that means
danger is near!

It's an Allosaurus! Stegosaurus
swings her spiked tail to defend herself.

She **pierces** the Allosaurus' skin.

He is hurt, but doesn't stop fighting.

The bony bumps on Stegosaurus' skin protect her. She swings her tail again, hitting the Allosaurus.

He is hurt and falls down.

Stegosaurus escapes!

The Search Continues

Stegosaurus finds a shady spot
under a tree to rest.

Soon, she has cooled off enough
to search for more food and make
her way home.

As she makes her way back
to her nest, Stegosaurus finds a
new patch of ferns to eat.

An **ankylosaur** is already
eating them! Luckily, there are
plenty of ferns to share.

New Babies

Finally, Stegosaurus arrives back at her nest. To her surprise, several of her eggs have hatched! Stegosaurus is a mom! The babies don't look like Stegosaurus yet, but they will.

It's the end of the day. The sun
sets and Stegosaurus is tired.

She looks around. All is
safe and quiet. She falls asleep
near her babies.

Glossary

Allosaurus: a dinosaur that despite its size, is thought to have been a speedy hunter, running up to 20 miles per hour

ankylosaur: a dinosaur with tough skin that was covered with bony plates. It could swing its clubbed tail to protect itself from predators.

beak: the Stegosaurus' mouth part, used to eat plants

Brachiosaurus: a very large dinosaur with nostrils on top of its head. Its front legs were longer than its back legs.

fern: a plant that has roots, stems and fronds, but no flowers

pierce: to make a hole in something

predator: an animal that captures other animals for food

About the Stegosaurus (STEG-o-SAW-rus)

Stegosaurus lived on earth about 200 million years ago, in a time known as the Jurassic period. It was an herbivore, which means it ate only plants.

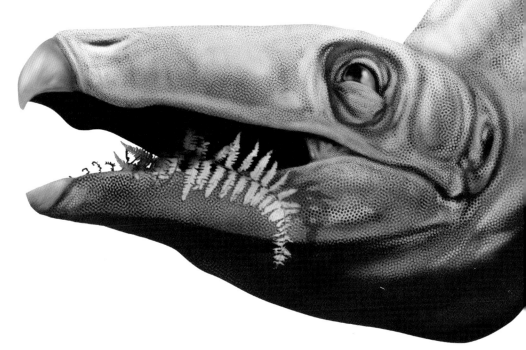

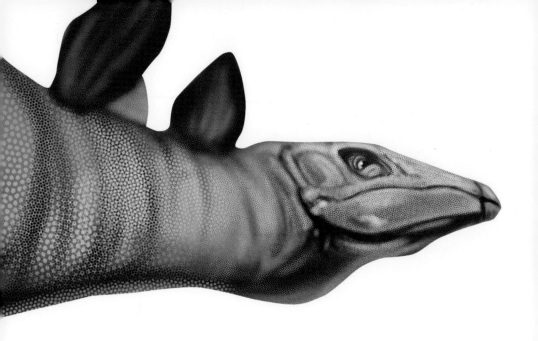

Stegosaurus weighed about two tons—that's 4,480 pounds! *Stegosaurus* was a very big dinosaur, but its head was very small, just 18 inches long. Its brain was only about the size of a walnut. Having such a tiny brain meant that *Stegosaurus* was not a very smart dinosaur.

The large bony plates on the back of *Stegosaurus* were used for defense and to help control the dinosaur's body temperature.

For Additional Learning

Help your child better understand the story by assisting them in collecting materials and following these instructions to complete extension activities.

Prehistoric Pizza

Herbivores like Stegosaurus only ate plants. Learn how to make your very own veggie pizza that any herbivore would love!

Always make sure to check with your adult caregiver before making a new snack to ensure that you are not exposed to food allergens.

What you will need:

- 1 small jar pizza sauce
- 1 package of ready-made pizza crust (individual size)
- 1 cup grated mozzarella cheese
- 1 cookie sheet or baking stone
- Your favorite toppings such as:
    - olives
    - onions
    - peppers
    - broccoli
    - pineapple
    - mushrooms

Directions:

1. Ask an adult to preheat the oven to 450 degrees Fahrenheit.

2. Spoon a layer of pizza sauce onto the crust and spread it around evenly.

3. Sprinkle cheese on top of the sauce.

4. Make a dinosaur face by arranging your favorite vegetable toppings as eyes, a nose and even a mouth with sharp pointy teeth!

5. With the help of an adult, place the pizza on a cookie sheet or baking stone. Bake the pizza for eight to ten minutes, or until the cheese begins to bubble. When it's ready, remove from the oven and let it cool for a few minutes.

Enjoy your prehistoric pizza!

Create a Reading Journal

After your child reads the story, ask him or her to tell you about it using words, pictures or both. He or she can create a reading journal, write about or draw a favorite part of the story, or retell the story in his or her own words. These exercises build reading comprehension skills as well as basic writing skills.

Lead the Way,
Velociraptor!

Based on text by Dawn Bentley
Illustrated by Karen Carr

Published by Soundprints™, an imprint of Palm Publishing, Norwalk, Connecticut USA
www.palmkids.com

Editors: Barbie Heit & Samantha Schlemm
Book design: Katie Sears & Scott Variano

First Edition 2012
10 9 8 7 6 5 4 3 2 1

Acknowledgements:

Carol LeBlanc, *Vice President*, Smithsonian Enterprises
Brigid Ferraro, *Director of Licensing*, Smithsonian Enterprises

Our special thanks to Ellen Nanney and Kealy Wilson at the Smithsonian Institution's Licensing Division for their help in the creation of this book.
Our very special thanks to Dr. Mike Brett-Surman of the Smithsonian Institution's National Museum of Natural History for his curatorial review of this title.

Library of Congress Control Number: 2012940525

Table of Contents

Small & Speedy 5

Hunting 8

Still Hungry 17

Resting. 24

Always Ready! 26

Glossary 28

About the Velociraptor 29

Small & Speedy

Velociraptor is a small, smart, speedy dinosaur. He is always looking for adventure.

Standing high up on a **cliff**, Velociraptor looks for others from his **pack**.

He uses his claws to climb
higher up the rocky hill, so
he can see farther.

Hunting

He spots other Velociraptors from his pack and joins them.

They will **hunt** for food together.

Velociraptor runs quickly
across the hot, dry land.

His stiff tail helps him **balance**
and make quick turns as he
looks for a meal.

Velociraptor finds an **ornithomimosaur**. The ornithomimosaur is very big, but Velociraptor is smart.

He can catch the ornithomimosaur
by working with his pack.

The Velociraptor pack circles
around the big dinosaur. Then
they attack him from all sides.

The ornithomimosaur can't
fight off all of the Velociraptors
at the same time.

16

Still Hungry

After the ornithomimosaur hunt, the Velociraptors are still hungry! They see an **Oviraptor** eating some eggs nearby. The pack scares the Oviraptor away and eats all of the eggs.

The Velociraptor pack is on
the move again. There are many
animals at a stream nearby.

When they see the pack, the
animals scatter. Everyone is afraid
of Velociraptors.

Velociraptor runs ahead of
his pack. A **Protoceratops** and
an Oviraptor are fighting.

The two dinosaurs see the pack
coming and run away in fear. No one
wants to fight a pack of Velociraptors.

A little mammal runs by
Velociraptor. He is tired,
but not too tired to trap it.
Velociraptor is a good hunter!

Resting

With a full belly, Velociraptor
lies down to rest.

He cleans his claws. They are
his most important tools.

Always Ready!

It's been a long day. As the
sun goes down, the Velociraptors
rest for the night.

Before long, the pack will leap
into action again. These dinosaurs
are always ready for adventure.

Glossary

balance: to keep steady

cliff: a high steep surface made of rock, earth or ice

ornithomimosaur: a fast-running dinosaur with very long legs, a long neck and a long beak

hunt: to chase and capture animals for food

Oviraptor: a dinosaur with long, slender legs and huge hands with three long, slender fingers

pack: a group of animals that live and hunt together

Protoceratops: a horned dinosaur with a strong beak, used to tear and chew plants

About the Velociraptor
(vel-OS-i-RAP-tor)

Velociraptor lived about 75 million years ago. It weighed up to 50 pounds and was just three feet tall. That's probably smaller than you!

Velociraptor was small compared to many dinosaurs that lived during its time. But *Velociraptor* had a big brain for its size and was very smart, which made it a great hunter.

Velociraptor could run up to 25 miles per hour and change direction quickly by swinging its tail. It was able to catch almost any dinosaur it chased.

For Additional Learning

Help your child better understand the story by assisting them in collecting materials and following these instructions to complete extension activities.

Make Your Own Dinosaur Eggs

What you will need:

- 2 ½ cups flour
- 1 ½ cups salt
- 1 cup sand
- 1 container to mix in (bowl, bucket, etc.)
- Water
- Plastic dinosaurs

Directions:

1. In your container, mix together the dirt, flour, salt and sand.

2. Slowly stir in water until your mixture becomes clay-like and begins to hold together.

3. Choose your favorite plastic dinosaur and mold the dough around it in the shape of an egg. Repeat this process with other dinosaur toys.

4. Let your dinosaur eggs dry until they harden. This may take more than one day depending on the weather.

5. Once your eggs are completely dry, you can crack them open like a paleontologist, or ask someone to hide them for you and do a dinosaur scavenger hunt!

Create a Reading Journal

After your child reads the story, ask him or her to tell you about it using words, pictures or both. He or she can create a reading journal, write about or draw a favorite part of the story, or retell the story in his or her own words. These exercises build reading comprehension skills as well as basic writing skills.

Snack Time, Tyrannosaurus rex!

Based on text by Dawn Bentley
Illustrated by Karen Carr

SMITHSONIAN INSTITUTION

Published by Soundprints™, an imprint of Palm Publishing,
Norwalk, Connecticut USA
www.palmkids.com

Editors: Barbie Heit & Samantha Schlemm
Book design: Katie Sears & Scott Variano

First Edition 2012
10 9 8 7 6 5 4 3 2 1

Acknowledgements:

Carol LeBlanc, *Vice President*, Smithsonian Enterprises
Brigid Ferraro, *Director of Licensing*, Smithsonian Enterprises

Our special thanks to Ellen Nanney and Kealy Wilson at the Smithsonian
Institution's Licensing Division for their help in the creation of this book.
Our very special thanks to Dr. Mike Brett-Surman of the Smithsonian
Institution's National Museum of Natural History for his curatorial review.

Library of Congress Control Number: 2012940526

Table of Contents

It's Tyrannosaurus rex 5

A Good Smell 11

Ready to Fight 16

Ouch! 23

An Eruption 26

Glossary 28

About the Tyrannosaurus rex 29

It's Tyrannosaurus rex!

The birds are chirping and the insects are buzzing. Animals splash in a stream. Then, a loud pounding sound fills the air. It's Tyrannosaurus rex!

Tyrannosaurus rex is very
hungry. She hopes to find
something good to eat.

She heads out to **hunt** for
her snack.

A group of **Quetzalcoatlus** flies
through the sky.

Tyrannosaurus rex snaps at one of
the flying **reptiles**, but she misses.
The Quetzalcoatlus flies away.

A Good Smell

After losing the Quetzalcoatlus, Tyrannosaurus rex smells a snack! Something moves in the stream. Tyrannosaurus rex goes toward the stream for a closer look.

As she heads into the water,
Tyrannosaurus rex almost steps on a
crocodile hiding in the **reeds**.

The crocodile is not her snack!

Further up the stream,
Tyrannosaurus rex sees what
smelled so good.

It's a **Triceratops**. Tyrannosaurus rex chases him!

Ready to Fight

The Triceratops is ready to
fight Tyrannosaurus rex.
He points his horns at her.

She decides to look for an easier
meal. Even powerful dinosaurs
know when not to fight.

Tyrannosaurus rex continues
her search for food. She sees a baby
Ankylosaurus hiding in the rocks.

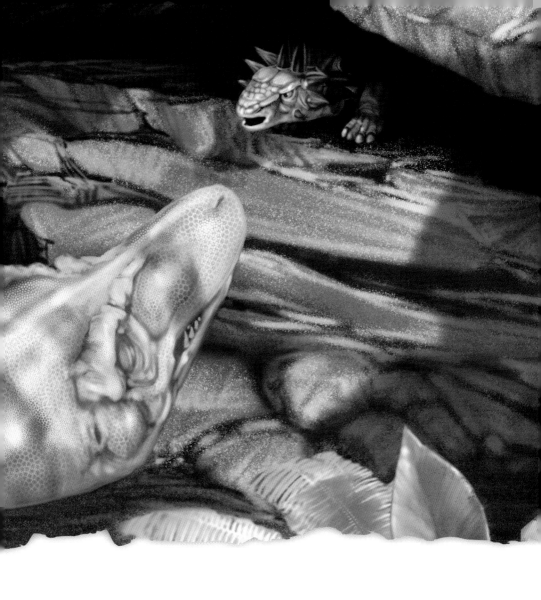

She tries to reach him, but her head is too big.

She snaps at the young
Ankylosaurus, but misses.

Tyrannosaurus rex's stomach
grumbles. She tries to push her
head in between the rocks.

22

Ouch!

Tyrannosaurus rex doesn't give up. She snaps at the baby again. This time she bites into a rock. *Crack!* She breaks one of her teeth! The Ankylosaurus quickly runs away.

Tyrannosaurus rex's luck finally changes when she finds an **Anatotitan**.

It took a long time to find her tasty
snack. Now, she can catch and eat
this slow-moving dinosaur.

An Eruption

Just as Tyrannosaurus rex
finishes eating, a **volcano** erupts!
Tyrannosaurus rex is powerful, but
even *she* is afraid of a volcano.

Tyrannosaurus rex runs to a safe
place so she can once again be
the most powerful thing of all!

Glossary

Anatotitan: one of the last dinosaurs. Its most unusual feature was its beak which looked like the mouth or bill of a duck.

Ankylosaurus: a dinosaur with tough skin, covered with bony plates. It could swing its clubbed tail to protect itself from predators.

hunt: to find and capture an animal for food

Quetzalcoatlus: a huge flying reptile. It was the largest flying animal ever found.

reed: a tall, slender, grassy plant

reptile: a four-legged animal that lays an egg with a hard shell

Triceratops: the biggest and heaviest of the horned dinosaurs. It weighed 11 tons and was nearly 30 feet long!

volcano: a mountain from which hot liquid, gas and ash erupt, or burst out

About the Tyrannosaurus rex
(tye-RAN-oh-saur-us rex)

Tyrannosaurus rex roamed the earth 65 million years ago. *Tyrannosaurus rex* was the biggest meat-eating dinosaur on land at that time.

Taller than a school bus, it weighed up to eight tons—more than two large elephants!

Table of Contents

Breakfast Time 5

Be Careful! 12

Tyrannosaurus rex! 19

The Herd Helps Out 22

Glossary 28

About the Triceratops 29

Breakfast Time

One sunny day, Triceratops sets out with his **herd** to look for food in the prehistoric forest.

Triceratops hears a noise in the trees. He sneaks up for a closer look.

As he moves away from his herd
he sees two **Pachycephalosaurus**
fighting.

While he watches the fight,
Triceratops feels his tummy rumble.

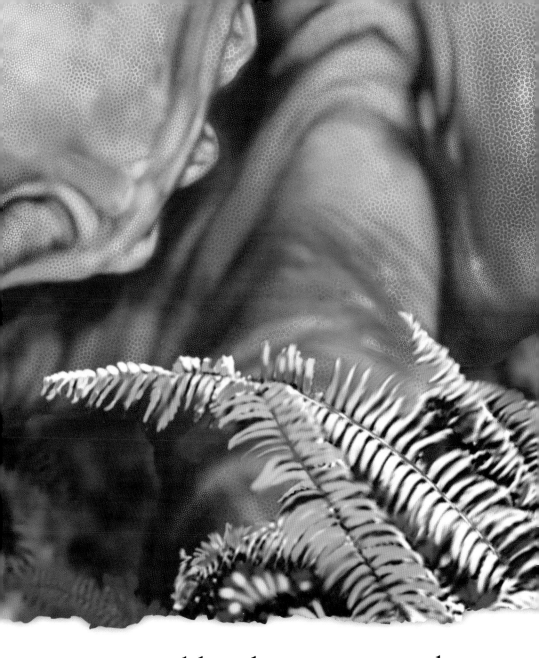

Ferns would make a great snack.
He breaks off a stem from a fern
on the ground.

Triceratops eats until he is full. When he looks up, the other Triceratops are not with him! He is not safe alone. He must find his herd.

Be Careful!

Hungry, flying **reptiles** circle above Triceratops. He runs and hides. The flying reptiles find something else to eat.

Triceratops is safe for now, but danger lies ahead.

After the long chase, Triceratops stops near a stream.

His herd is still nowhere in sight.

Triceratops is tired. He finds
a shady place to rest.

As soon as he drifts to sleep
a loud noise scares him awake.
What could it be?

18

Tyrannosaurus Rex!

It's a hungry Tyrannosaurus rex! Triceratops would make a tasty meal.

Tyrannosaurus rex is a meat eater.
She has big, sharp teeth!

Triceratops is afraid, but he does
his best to be brave.

The Herd Helps Out

Triceratops is much smaller
than Tyrannosaurus rex, but he is
ready to fight.

He points his horns at Tyrannosaurus rex. Suddenly, the ground shakes!

It is the Triceratops herd!

They are here to help him.

Tyrannosaurus rex cannot win
this fight. She stomps away.

Back in the group, Triceratops
is safe again.

From now on, Triceratops will
stay with his herd as they search for
tasty plants to eat together.

Glossary

herd: a large number of animals of the same kind that travel as a group

horns: hard, pointed body parts on animals, reptiles, birds, fish or insects

fern: a plant that has roots, stems and fronds, but no flowers

Pachycephalosaurus: a dinosaur with a very thick skull. The males may have had head-butting contests.

reptile: a four-legged animal that lays an egg with a hard shell

Tyrannosaurus rex: the biggest meat-eating dinosaur that ever lived on land

About the Triceratops
(try-SAIR-uh-tops)

Triceratops lived on earth about 65 million years ago! *Triceratops* means "three-horned face." All *Triceratops* had horns. Their big horns and bony neck shields would scare some enemies and protect them from others.

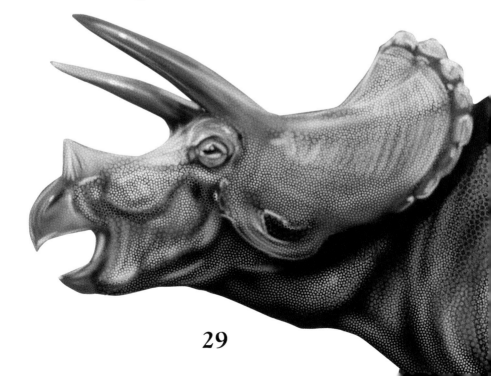

Triceratops was the biggest and heaviest of the horned dinosaurs. It weighed 11 tons and was nearly 30 feet long!

Triceratops was a plant-eater and had a strong, sharp beak that helped it bite through thick stems and branches.

For Additional Learning

Help your child better understand the story by assisting them in collecting materials and following these instructions to complete extension activities.

How Big is a Dinosaur?

What you will need:

- Measuring tape
- A large outdoor space (such as a park or football field)
- 2 Placeholders (such as orange traffic cones)

Directions:

Triceratops were about 30 feet long. To help your child understand how big they really were, go to a large, open outdoor space.

1. Use a measuring tape to help your child measure and mark 30 feet out on the field with a placeholder.
2. Have your child lie down on the ground next to the 30 foot measurement and measure their height.
3. Mark your child's height next to the *Triceratops'* with another placeholder and compare the two. Ask your child: Is the dinosaur bigger or smaller than you?
4. Repeat these steps with other dinosaurs like *Tyrannosaurus rex* (40 feet) and *Velociraptor* (3 feet). Ask your child: Were you surprised by the size of any dinosaurs?

Create a Reading Journal

After your child reads the story, ask him or her to tell you about it using words, pictures or both. He or she can create a reading journal, write about or draw a favorite part of the story or retell the story in his or her own words. These exercises build reading comprehension skills as well as basic writing skills.